The Adventures of Sam Pig

The May Queen
Alison Uttley

Illustrated by Graham Percy

faber and faber
LONDON · BOSTON

First published in 1942
by Faber and Faber Limited
3 Queen Square London WC1N 3AU
This edition first published in 1989

Printed in Great Britain by
W.S. Cowell Ltd Ipswich

British Library Cataloguing in Publication Data is available

ISBN 0–571–15296–1

The May Queen

Brock the Badger sat in the kitchen one day of early spring, with the little pigs round him.

'Show us your pocket-book, Brock. Tell us about the feast days coming,' they pleaded.

'It was such a long cold winter,' said Sam. 'I thought it would never end. I'm glad there are feast days.'

Brock took the old leather-backed book from his pocket and turned the pages so that the little pigs could look at the pictures.

'Daffodil Day in March,' said Brock. 'And here's April. April Fool's Day, when we all play tricks. Swallow Day, when the first swallow comes. Nightingale Day, when the little brown bird sings. Cuckoo Day, when our old friend flies over the sea to our woods. All those festivals for April.'

'Cowslip Day, when the first cowslip is out,' added Sam Pig, leaning over Brock's shoulder and pointing to a picture of the flowers painted in gay colours on the brown page.

Brock turned over, and showed them a fine picture with many a gay scene.

'That is a day when men as well as animals have a feast. What is it? Who can tell me?'

'May Day,' they all shouted together.

'Yes, May Day, when the children dance round the Maypole. May Day, when the cart-horses are decorated and their shoes blacked and polished. Then Sally the mare will have her mane plaited, with straw tassels standing up in a row, and her tail brushed in a wave with little straw plaiting and ribbons down the centre. It's Sally's day too.'

'The cart will be decorated, won't it, Brock?' asked Ann.

'Yes. Everything at the farm will be spick and span, washed and clean, polished and brushed for May Day,' said Brock.

'And everything in the house of the four pigs must be clean and fresh for May Day too,' said Ann.

'Yes. We'll have a May Day feast like the farm.'

On the Eve of May Day Sam Pig went over to the farm to talk to Sally the mare. She stood in the stable, while the boy plaited her mane and tail in many plaits to make it curly for the next day. Her fetlocks were washed and combed, her coat

groomed. The ribbons and rosettes and straw hung near, ready for May Day. Sam slipped quietly away and went to the cowhouses. He found everyone excited and gay. The cows were going to be let into the big meadow the next morning, and they were talking of the sweetness of the grass there, and the taste of the spring that ran through the field, and the feeling of comfort of the old tree stump where they rubbed their backs and sides. They were looking forward to May Day.

The little pigs in the pig-cote were squealing so loudly they didn't hear Sam's step as he crept up to the wall and looked over at them.

'Oh Sam! How you startled us!' they cried. 'Do you know what day it is tomorrow?'

'May Day,' said Sam proudly. 'I know!'

'Yes, and we are going to be let into the little orchard, so that we can rootle among the trees. My! It will be a treat after being shut in the pig-cote yard for so long. The grass is thick and cold, and we shall scratch our backs on the trees, and gallop around like circus pigs. We shall dig and wallow to our hearts' content on May Day.'

Sam walked on, to visit the pasture where the sheep and lambs were feeding. The sheep called to their little ones, who frisked and danced on their hind legs like ballet girls.

'Oh, Sam Pig! It's May Day tomorrow,' they bleated. 'Our lambs are going to race from the oak tree to the white gate. It's the May Day race, and for many a year the lambs have run that race.'

'Yes. I can see a little deep path,' said Sam, looking at the ground where a tiny track led from tree to gate.

'We ran there in our childhood. Our mothers ran too. Now our children are going to race. The winner will be the Queen of the lambs,' said the sheep.

So Sam went through the farm and everywhere he heard tales of the May Day festival.

Then he saw two children coming from the house with a basket. He crouched low under the hedge out of their way, but he could hear their voices ringing across the field with joy.

'We'll gather cowslips and bluebells from Puwit Meadow, and Jack-by-the-hedge from Cuckoo Meadow, and some primroses for my hair,' said the little girl.

'And we'll get some fresh branches of larch for an archway to hold over you, and some young beech leaves too,' said the little boy.

'And daffodils from the riverside, and forget-me-nots if we can find any out yet.'

'And a tulip from the garden, and some wild cherry from the wood,' added the boy.

They ran with skipping steps over the meadow, and the girl began to sing as she picked the blossoms and filled her basket.

'I shall be Queen of the May. I shall be Queen of the May.'

Sam Pig went home thoughtfully.

'What is Queen of the May?' he asked Brock.

'A little girl wears a crown of flowers and garlands. In some places they have a Crowning of the Queen, with dancers and all. They dance round the Maypole and sing a song,' said Brock.

'I should like to be Queen of the May,' said little Ann Pig.

'Yes,' said Sam. 'Ann is our prettiest little girl. She shall be the May Queen.'

'Hurrah!' cried Bill and Tom, as Ann blushed with pleasure. 'Let Ann be Queen of the May.'

'Very well,' said Brock, laughing at their eagerness. 'Ann Pig is our very own Queen of the May.'

At daybreak they were out in the woods to gather fresh flowers and branches with the dew upon them. They carried their trophies back to the garden and wove them into garlands and wreaths. They made a crown of cowslips for little Ann's head. They put a chain of bluebells round her neck. They gave her a bouquet to carry.

'She ought to wear a veil. A Queen has a veil hanging from her head,' said Sam, who knew all about these things.

He ran out and brought home a beautiful cobweb, shimmering with dewdrops. Brock breathed upon it, and the drops glittered like diamonds, with rainbow colours. They draped the web from Ann's crown so that the little gleaming drops hung about her face.

'A Queen! A beautiful Queen! Much prettier than an ordinary girl,' they cried, bowing to her, and they led Ann to the stream to look at herself.

They gave her a sceptre made of an ivy-covered wand, and twisted an archway of branches to hold over her.

'Am I really a May Queen?' asked Ann as Brock took his pipe out of his mouth to stare at her.

'Realer than real. A grand May Queen, little Ann,' said Brock, and he clapped his hands.

'But where are you going?' he asked as the four pigs walked down the garden path, Ann leading, with her veil hanging about her, and the others carrying bunches of flowers, and the archway of young beech.

'To show ourselves to Sally the mare, and Rosie the cow, and perhaps to Mollie the dairymaid, or to Farmer Greensleeves,' they said.

'That's all right,' said Brock. 'I thought you had some other plan in your foolish little noddles.'

They walked across the fields to the farm. In the big meadow the cows were frisking, eating the sweet grass, rubbing their sides against the well-known smooth tree trunk.

'I am the Queen of the May,' said Ann Pig.

The cows glanced at her, and turned away to their feeding, but Rosie, the red heifer, ran across the field to admire little Ann.

Quickly Ann picked a bunch of buttercups and wove them into a circlet. She threw the wreath over the cow's horns.

'There, Rosie. You too are a Queen of the May,' said she.

The little procession left the field and went to the pasture where the sheep gathered with their lambs.

'Who is the Queen of the lambs?' asked Ann Pig.

'The race is about to begin,' said a hurried, flustered mother, pushing her twins into the row with the crowd. Off they went, leaping and running, away from the old oak tree across the field to the white gate. Every sheep called to her youngling, and there was such a chorus of baas it was deafening. The lambs reached the white gate in a mob, and turned round, tearing helter-skelter, tumbling over one another, leaping over a ditch in the way, dancing on their neat little toes, waving their flags of tails.

'Run, little one, run,' cried every mother in the field.

'I am running, mother,' bleated the babies.

A little black lamb was the winner, and it ran to its mother to be nuzzled and petted.

'She shall be Queen of the lambs for May,' said Ann, and she crowned the lamb with a crown of daisies.

Then away went the four little pigs, with Ann in front wearing her chaplet of cowslips, and the others holding the arch of leaves over her veiled head.

They went to the orchard where the little pigs were rootling, and digging for roots.

'Here's the May Queen,' they cried, when they saw Ann. They all danced round an apple tree, which they called their Maypole, and Ann sat in the low branch singing with them.

Next they went to the farmyard where Sally the mare was standing, waiting for the farmer and the family. Sally's hoofs were blacked. Her tail was hanging free with a tiny plait of ribbons down the centre. Her frizzed mane was decorated with straw tassels, upright in a nodding row, and little stiff flowers stood between them. She wore all her horse brasses, shining like gold. The harness was clean and bright, and the cart had been washed and decorated with a bunch of flowers on each side.

'Queen Sally and Queen Ann,' said Sam Pig, looking at the mare in deep admiration. 'You are both Queens of the May.'

'There's another Queen coming out in a minute,' said Sally. 'But little Ann Pig is the best of all in my opinion. Of course I'm only an old mare, but I do know something about May Queens, and Ann is a beauty.'

The door opened and the farmer came out, dressed in his Sunday clothes. He carried the long whip with a ribbon tied to the handle. Behind him came the children and Mrs Green-sleeves. The little girl was dressed in white. She had a veil of muslin, and on her head a wreath of primroses and lilies. In her gloved hands she carried a large bouquet. She was indeed a proper little Queen of the May, with golden hair and pink cheeks and solemn face. She stared at Ann

Pig and Ann Pig stared back. After her ran the little boy, in his stiff Sunday clothes, with white collar and little blue tie. His face was red, polished with soap, and his hair was still wet with the washing he had had. He held a green larch bough, ready to put over his sister when they reached the village.

'Who the – ? What the – ? Who's this?' stammered the farmer, as he suddenly caught sight of the little pigs standing near Sally. 'Who's this May Queen?'

'Ann Pig, Sam Pig, Bill Pig and Tom,' said Sam, stepping forward.

'Bless my buttons! Bless my bottom sixpence! Bless my boots!' cried the farmer. 'Here's those wild little piglings, looking as nice as my own family. Well done! I'd take you with me to dance round the Maypole, but the cart will be full of us.'

'No, thank you,' said Ann, shrilly. 'I'm Queen of the May here, where I belong. Brock doesn't want us to go wandering.'

'Quite right,' nodded the farmer.

'Wife,' he called to Mrs Greensleeves. 'See here. Give this little May Queen a bite and a sup for May Day presents.'

The farmer's wife brought them cakes and milk and some sweet wizened apples from the apple chamber.

'It's time I was off, wife,' said the farmer, looking at his turnip watch. 'Come along, childer, and climb in the cart. We shall be late for Maypole dancing if we stay any longer.'

The little girl and boy climbed in, and the farmer's wife squeezed in after them. There certainly wasn't room for four little pigs as well.

'Gee up, Sally. Come along Sally lass,' chirruped the farmer, waving his ribboned whip round his head. The cavalcade started, with jingling of bells and tinkling of brasses, with nodding flowers and plumes and ribbons.

'Good-bye! Good-bye!' called the little pigs.

'A happy May Day,' called the children, and away they went.

'Time to go home,' said Sam. 'Brock will wonder where we are.'

'I wish we could dance round the Maypole,' said Ann, as they set off across the fields, running, with the veil tucked up and the flowers fluttering their petals.

Brock stood at the gate waiting for them, and when they went up the garden path there grew a Maypole in the middle of the grass. It was a tall pole of hawthorn, with flowers covering it, and long ribbons of woven grasses hanging down.

'Each take a ribbon and dance round the Maypole. That's the way to do it. In and out and roundabout,' said Brock.

He took a whistle pipe out of his pocket and

whistled a lively air, and the little pigs danced their Maypole dance, twisting the ribbons until they were in a tangle of knots.

They hung their wreaths and crown in the Maypole, and went into the kitchen. What a feast lay there! The good old Badger had been cooking all the time they had been Maying. He had set the table and spread out all the good things for them. There were bannocks and pikelets and oatcakes and barm dumplings, fried in the frying pan, baked on the stone girdle, as well as stuffed eggs and apple pie.

'Here's to the May Queen, and may she live long, and dance every May Day till the earth dances too,' said Brock, holding up a glass of cowslip wine and toasting the little May Queen.

'And here's to Old Brock, and may he live for ever,' said Sam.

'Here's to all of us, and all of you wherever you are,' said Brock again, and he drank to the whole wide world.